The Prodigal Son

A Cartoon Bible Story

The Prodigal Son

A Cartoon Bible Story

by Bill Walsh

With an Afterword for Parents and Teachers
by
Dr. Charlie Shedd

Sheed Andrews and McMeel, Inc.
Subsidiary of Universal Press Syndicate
Kansas City

The "Cartoon Bible Stories Series" is edited with an afterword by Dr. Charlie Shedd. Future selections will include stories appropriate for a better understanding by children of their faith.
Already released are:
Jonah and the Whale
Noah and the Ark

The Prodigal Son copyright © 1977 by Sheed Andrews and McMeel, Inc.
Afterword copyright © 1977 by Dr. Charlie Shedd.

All rights reserved. Printed in the United States of America. No part of this book may be used or reproduced in any manner whatsoever without written permission except in the case of reprints in the context of reviews. For information write Sheed Andrews and McMeel, Inc., 6700 Squibb Road, Mission, Kansas 66202.

Library of Congress Cataloging in Publication Data

Walsh, Bill.
   The prodigal son.

   (A Cartoon Bible story)
   SUMMARY: A cartoon version of the parable of the prodigal son who, after squandering his inheritance, returns home to his forgiving father.
   1. Prodigal son (Parable)—Caricatures and cartoons—Juvenile literature. [1. Prodigal son (Parable) 2. Parables. 3. Bible stories—N.T. 4. Cartoons and comics] I. Title.
BT378.P8W24   226'.8   77-1146
ISBN 0-8362-0693-2

A MAN HAD TWO SONS.

BUT ONE DAY---

"I'VE BEEN THINKING, BROTHER, WHY DO WE KNOCK OURSELVES OUT EVERY DAY UNDER THIS BLAZING SUN? LET'S ASK DAD FOR OUR CUT OF THE LOOT AND GO SEE SOME LIFE."

"NO, IT IS MY DUTY TO SERVE FATHER. I WILL STAY HERE AND WORK HIS FIELDS."

NOW HEAR THIS! WE HAVE A STORY BUILDING HERE.

SHORTLY AFTERWARD---

WHAT ARE YOU DOING HERE? WHY ARE YOU NOT IN THE FIELDS?

I'VE HAD IT, DAD. GIVE ME MY SHARE OF THE BREAD; I WANT TO GO OUT AND SEE SOME ACTION.

GET THIS NOW, THE FATHER REPRESENTS GOD, SEE, AND THE SON IS MAN.

UNTIL THE PRODIGAL* SON COMES TO A DISTANT CITY.

I DON'T KNOW ABOUT OTHER CAMELS, BUT, I'D LIKE A GLASS OF WATER.

*SPENDTHRIFT

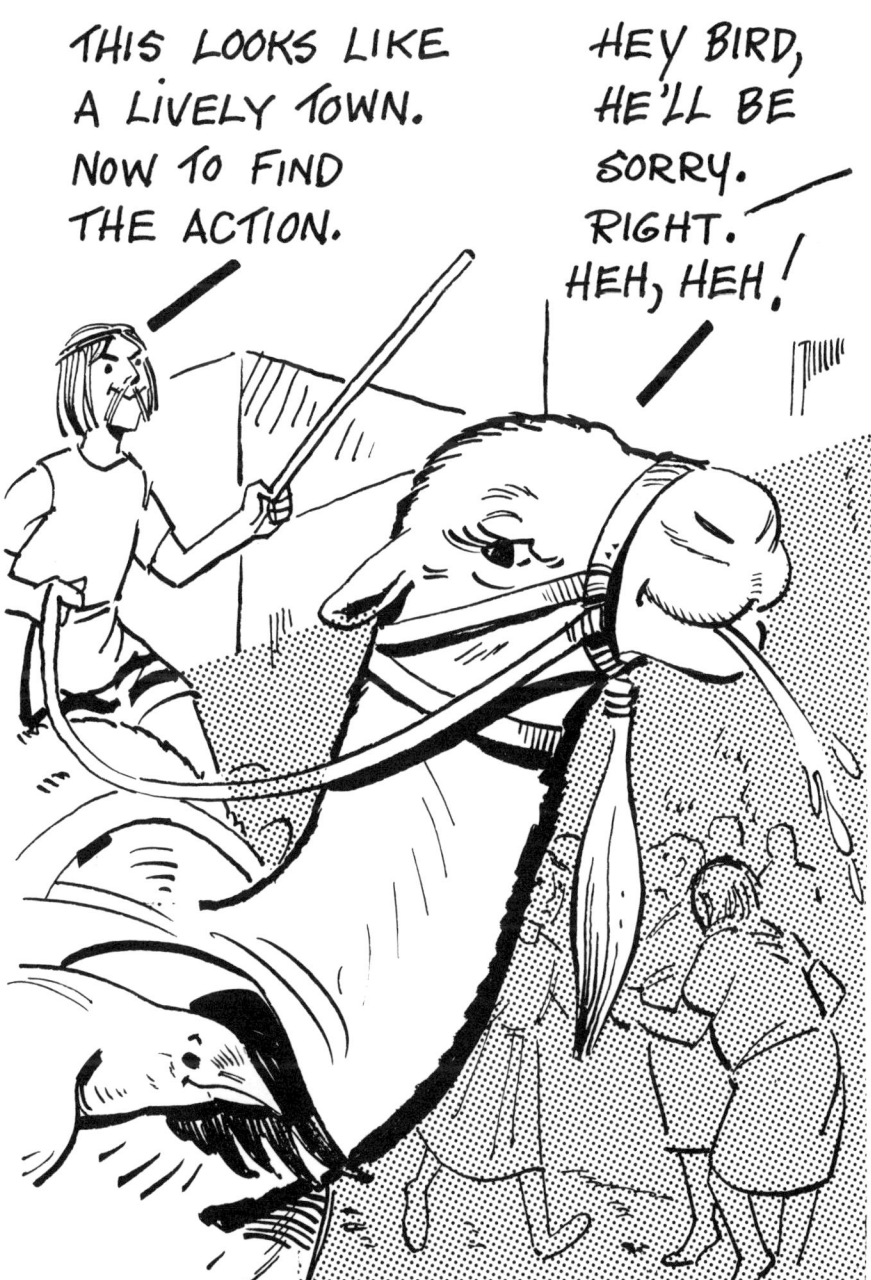

AND SO THE ENTOURAGE MOVES ON TO A NEW TOWN.

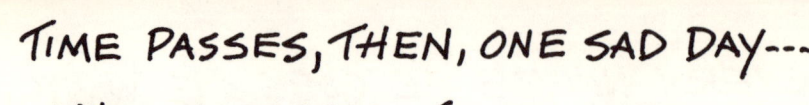

AWAY-AWAY! I NEED A STRONG MAN TO DO HEAVY WORK, YOU HAVE THE LOOK OF A WASTREL.

BUT DON'T YOU REMEMBER ME? YOU WERE IN THE CROWD THAT FOLLOWED ME.

BEAT IT!

THE WORK WAS HARD, THE FOOD NOT THE BEST.

IT'S THE WASTREL! I MUST HURRY TO TELL THE FATHER THAT HIS SON IS RETURNING.

53

WHAT! WASTING TIME ON THAT NO-GOODNICK. HE'S PROBABLY BROKE AND CAME CRAWLING BACK HOME. THERE'LL BE NO CELEBRATING ON MY PART.

THE FATHER IS SUMMONED BY THE SERVANT, ISAAC.

70

Afterword for Parents and Teachers

by Dr. Charlie Shedd
TALE OF TWO SONS
A STUDY FOR THE FAMILY TOGETHER

1. The Prodigal Son—God Never Quits Loving Us. His name was Flipper and on this night I am telling you about now, he crawled up onto my lap. It had not been one of his better days. He had fought with his sister, been obnoxious at school. (That's what his teacher indicated when we met her at the grocery store.) And his mother wondered only one thing when I got home from the office: Could she take off for an hour and just go somewhere? Anywhere. So she went. And after thirty minutes of him, I could understand fully why she made her request.

Then we got him ready for bed. Aren't they precious, fresh, clean, and on their way to eight hours of surcease? Maybe ten.

Then came that moment I will never forget. Ready for his story, he snuggled close and asked, "Daddy, could I ever do anything so bad that you would quit loving me?"

What do you think I answered? You're right. I said exactly what you would say.

"No way. Chances zero."

Jesus said that God loves us more than we love our children. In fact, said He, the extent of earthly parents' love for their own is only a glimmer of God's never-ending love for us.

If by some queer work of circumstance we had to give up all but one chapter of our Bible, Luke 15 is the keeper. Troops, let's have another look at it.

Was there ever a better storyteller than Jesus? None! Yet the drama of his parables, the way they grip us is not the most important thing. The most important thing is what his stories have to tell us of our God. And this one tells us that God is like a father who never gives up. Every night he goes out to the end of the road hoping that his boy will come home.

When the youngest son said, "Father, I want my share," the law said he could have it. That's what the scholars tell us. So he took it and off he went. But when it was gone, he thought of the one good place he'd known. Home. And when he arrived, broke, barefoot maybe, beat, he didn't even get a chance to make his speech. He rehearsed it well, "Father, I am no longer worthy to be called your son" (Luke 15:19).

Why didn't he have a chance to say his thing?

Reason: Luke 15:20. Focus now on these three words, "the father ran."

Let's talk about this, gang. Wouldn't it have been fair for him to stand behind the door, arms akimbo, and say, "Let him knock awhile. Remember how he insulted me, embarrassed me with his remarks. Now he's wasted what I gave him. Let's see if he's sincere."

Why didn't he do that?

You're right. It's because God, the Father, is like him—Luke 15:22-24, "Let us eat and be merry. For this my son was dead, and is alive again. He was lost, and is found."

So just in case you ever worry whether your mom and dad are going to love you no matter what, *always* is a long time. For ever and ever we'll never stop caring for you.

Question: Do you think a child who knows this is more likely_____ or less likely_____ to go to a far country?

What difference do you think it would make in our behavior if we really believed what Jesus is telling us about God?

Prayer:

Thank you, heavenly Father, for loving us no matter what. Help us to love you back like you love us. Forever.
                                  Amen.

A STUDY FOR THE FAMILY TOGETHER

2. *Do You Think You Are Better Than Other People?* They were advertising a Christian college. Obviously the purpose was to fortify worried parents. "This is the place. Hurry on down. Don't worry your insecure heads one moment longer. We have the perfect spiritual setting for future saints of the Lord."

And the sign read: "SEVEN MILES FROM ANY KNOWN SIN."

What do you think? Okay? If not, why not?

The Scripture for our study now is Luke 15:25-32, "neither transgressed I at any time thy commandment." He was right. He had stayed home. He had worked hard. He had saved his money. He hadn't "wasted his substance in riotous living." So, what's the problem? The problem is that he looks so unattractive in his righteousness. Call it pious, pompous, judgmental. By any other name it turns us off. But there is another more serious problem here. His idea of transgression was much too limited. This character would have made an excellent president "SEVEN MILES FROM ANY KNOWN SIN."

If you were choosing the prodigal or the elder brother for a friend, who would you rather know?

Are there any clues in the passage, "He was in the fields" (Luke 15:25)? Suppose he was tired? Do you ever blow up when you're weary? Couldn't we make it a rule around here:

1. To count to ten;
2. To sleep on it;
3. To table the matter until we're rested.

"He was angry and would not go in" (Luke 15:28). Did you ever miss a good time because you were in a pout? Any secrets to share? How can we snap ourselves out of it before the party is over?

Verse 28 also says, "Therefore went his father out and entreated him." Remember in our study of the Prodigal Son we said, "God never quits loving us." What does this verse tell us about our heavenly father? Loud and clear it says, "He loves us even when we're not nice."

Jesus talked often about the sins of the spirit. Name some. Altogether now: "God never quits loving us."

Thank you, God.

Books in the Cartoon Stories for New Children Series:

What is God's Area Code?
A Kelly-Duke Book by Jack Moore
$4.95 (cloth); $2.25 (paper)

Joanie
A Doonesbury Book by G. B. Trudeau
$4.95 (cloth); $2.45 (paper)

"Francine, Your Face Would Stop a Clock"
A Miss Peach Book by Mell Lazarus
$4.95 (cloth); $2.45 (paper)

We'll Take It from Here, Sarge
A Doonesbury Book by G. B. Trudeau
$2.45 (paper)

Let's See if Anyone Salutes
A Steve Canyon Book by Milton Caniff
$2.45 (paper)

The Smoke from Gasoline Alley
A Gasoline Alley Book by Dick Moores
$2.45 (paper)

If I Quit Baseball, Will You Still Love Me?
A Tank McNamara Book by Jeff Millar and Bill Hinds
$2.25 (paper)

The Pogo Candidature
A Pogo Book by Walt and Selby Kelly
$1.95 (paper)

Shoot, Tank, Shoot!
A Tank McNamara Book by Jeff Millar and Bill Hinds
$1.95 (paper)

If you are unable to obtain these books from your local bookseller, they may be ordered from the publisher. Enclose payment with order.

Sheed Andrews and McMeel, Inc.
6700 Squibb Road
Mission, Kansas 66202